THE NINETEEN YEARS OF SAMANTHA

SAMANTHA'S JOURNEY UNTIL 19

VANDANA SAHU

Made with ♥ on the Notion Press Platform
www.notionpress.com

TO MY PARENTS;

WHO ARE MY STRENGTH

Contents

Preface

"The nineteen years of Samantha" is a book by VANDANA SAHU, who uses the pen name Samantha.

This book emphasizes that success isn't just about reaching a grand, overarching goal. It's equally, if not more, important to celebrate and value the small wins, the daily achievements that contribute to growth. These small victories shape a person's character, personality, kindness, and honesty.

This book, written in an accessible style, tells the story of Samantha's journey up to the age of 19. A key element of her success at each stage of her life was the unwavering support of her father, who was a constant presence and driving force behind her achievements.

ONE
SAMANTHA'S CHILDHOOD

Born on october 19, 2005. She possessed a vivacious spirit mirrored in her bright, curly hair and the warm depths of her brown eyes. Samantha is the middle child of her parents. Her father was a vehicle mechanic and her mother was a housewife.

On the first day of parallel school, she hit her teacher and ran away home. Initially, she was not very good at her studies that's why she had to repeat UKG class.

Samantha's accident

Unfortunately, at the age of two Samantha once involved in a severe accident while she was at a party she and her family was invited to. She was very badly injured and was bleeding profusely, her grandfather brought her home and her entire family was very sad and very tense about her. Samantha and her family faced a moment where it was a matter of life and death because the situation was very critical but, Samantha luckily survived.

However, a period of six to seven years elapsed before she fully recuperated, owing to her persistent difficulty in ambulating with proper functionality of her lower limbs. Her father used to massage her feet every day.

Samantha and family

Samantha grew up in a joint family and spent her most of the time with her cousins. Samantha had a cousin who couldn't hear or speak. She had to communicate with her through actions, and Samantha spent more time with her and communicate with her trough actions. Samantha, a free spirit even as a child, played outside a lot.

Samantha had one elder and one younger sister, with whom she frequently quarreled, mainly with her elder sister. She used to fight and then hide in the bathroom to avoid each other.

Her stubbornness

Samantha, in her formative years, exhibited a pronounced introversion, coupled with a volatile temper and a stubborn resistance to authority. She always determined to get anything she wanted.

"Once Samantha insisted to buy some fake nails from the fair, but no one at her home could take her. So, she asked her next-door neighbor's grandmother to go with her, just for a cheap five rupee packet of nails."

Samantha was a girl who insisted on participating in most school functions even when her family wasn't keep on it. 'Once Samantha got the role of swami Vivekananda in her school. At that time, her entire family was going to a wedding, except for her grandparents. However, she wasn't allowed to go because she was engaged in the role of swami Vivekananda, and she kept crying to go to the wedding'. Her stubbornness weighed heavily on her.

Samantha's school once planed a picnic and asked all the students for money. Samantha's parents refused. When the school was about to go for the picnic, Samantha cried and persuaded her grandfather to allow her to go on the picnic.

"No Matter What, Samantha was a stubborn girl but was her grandfather's darling".

Samantha was five year old when her younger sister was born and the third child was also a girl. In middle class families, there's a lot of societal pressure on parents to have a son, also in Samantha's whole family, her dad is the only one with all daughters. But Samantha's father considered himself as unique for having only daughters. The thought that they might not have a son had never truly entered their minds.

"They were convinced that whatever God provides is for the good".

Samantha's father was a man of decidedly modern sensibilities, their thinking far ahead of their time. Also they remained dedicated to their work until it was completed.

He held the belief that girls were equally capable, if not more so, than boys. They have consistently provided unwavering support for their Daughters aspirations and endeavors.

The societal pressure to have son was so prevalent because the dowry system was deeply entrenched, especially in northern India.

Now, Samantha is growing up slowly and is also becoming quite good at her studies. She and all her cousins used to go her aunt's place for tuition. She used to enjoy reading a lot there. She would often play hide and seek with them and try out many recipes and cakes, also her aunt used to teach them dance there. In All the houses, there was only a camera at aunt's place, with which her aunt's used to take their photos.

Camera picture

"Since childhood, Samantha had dreamt of becoming a pilot. However, she didn't realize the high cost of becoming a pilot until, she learned about it on internet. This discovery shattered her dream." But the same internet that shattered her dream showed her new paths.

Nevertheless, prior to this juncture, the struggles borne by Samantha's father were more formidable than her own.

Samantha's father exhibited remarkable patience, self-confidence, and perseverance. Despite having three daughters and a significant hiatus from formal education, he commenced preparations for government examinations at the age of thirty. At that time Samantha's dad shut down their shop for more than two years, and her grandfather covered all their expenses.

Samantha's grandfather was a ticket collector in the railways, and he provide immense support to everyone in the family.

"It is often asserted that the education of a single child can significantly alter the circumstances of a household. However, this situation is unique. In this particular instance, it was her father who transformed the family condition".

Both Samantha's father and uncle who began preparing, but it was her uncle who was selected in his very first attempt and Samantha's father couldn't.

Owing to this circumstance, his father endured considerable stress, exacerbated by his inability to provide for his family during this period of preparation. Samantha seen her father's youthful perseverance when he was thirty years old, but she did not recognize at the time due to her youthful innocence

Resuming one's academic pursuits after an extended hiatus proved to be an arduous endeavor.

Finally, Samantha's father demonstrated his capabilities in his ultimate endeavor. Coincidently, the day the paternal figure received the telephone call was the exact day the grandfather retired from his professional duties.

It made her whole family quite emotional, especially her grandfather, who had always been a tremendous support to his son. A few days later, his father joined as an assistant loco pilot in the Indian Railways in Karnataka.

Now, Samantha, her younger sister, mom and dad were supposed to go to Karnataka, except for the elder sister. This was because the language spoken there is different, Kannada, and she couldn't handle it, being in the higher class of school.

Samantha was very excited to go to Karnataka. She used to tell her school classmates that she was going out of town, which was a big deal. But she has no idea how much her life is about to change.

TWO

THE GREAT SHIFT IN SAMANTHA'S LIFE

Samantha had always wondered how people ventured beyond other cities and attained such enviable lifestyle; yet, this seemed confined to the realm of cinema, a distant reality in the actual world. But Samantha's life is also changing gradually in the same way, without her realizing it.

Samantha was ten years old when she and her family shifted to Sakleshpur. Sakleshpur was a hilly region resembling a lush green jungle, sometimes people also used to call it mini Ooty. As it had a six month rainy season and enjoyable weather year around.

Samantha had gotten into pioneer school and she was a bundle of nerves, but also really excited. However, what she actually faced "on the first day when Samantha went to school, no one in her class or even in the school could speak Hindi, except for one or two, generally Muslims." She was feeling very awkward in that class. The other students were making fun of her because for them, she was a girl who speak a different language, which was a new experience. The prevailing mode of communication amongst the student body was Kannada.

Samantha found it very difficult to wake up every morning, go to school, and face the students who made her feel insulted.

"Samantha who had arrived in Sakleshpur brimming with aspiration, novel ideas, and a zest for life, now encountered a formidable obstacle-the Kannada language. Kannada, being the first language of instruction, presented a significant challenge, adding a layer of complexity to her already unfamiliar surroundings. This, however, marked the true commencement of her journey, a period of adaptation and intellectual growth".

Samantha tried to build up her inner confidence. Without it, she wouldn't have had the courage to face her Classmates. This is the beginning of her journey to become more confident, because if we are confident, then we don't think about what others are thinking about us.

Value what we know because others don't know it, and similarly Samantha adopted a positive approach that she knows Hindi but others don't.

Samantha decided to take tuition for Kannada and started from zero. Where all the students had learned the Kannada letters in nursery, she studied those same latter in fifth grade. Learning Kannada seemed like such a difficult subject that all other subjects seemed very easy compared to it. She performed exceptionally well in all subjects but was held back by a single weak subject, that is Kannada.

Therefore, she spent most of her time on the Kannada subject.

During this time, Samantha made a friend who spoke Hindi. Samantha would talk to her and sit with her, and her friend would also teach her Kannada.

One day during games period, the games teacher called all the children to the ground to play Kho-Kho. Usually, only the selected students played Kho-Kho, that day teacher told Samantha to do dozing [running around, likely to warm up or practice] in Kho-Kho. She ran for two to three minutes, and no one could catch her. That day, the teacher selected her for the team, and this marked the beginning of Samantha's journey with Kho-Kho. Before that, she didn't even know what Kho-Kho was.

Everything was going smoothly, but then Samantha's friend announced she was moving to Banglore and leaving school. After her friend left school, Samantha was feeling very lonely. But this time Samantha is no longer new to her classmates, she started to both speak and write Kannada a little bit, so she started interacting with other classmate as well.

Samantha worked very hard to learn Kannada, from letters to word, and then to sentences. Upon entering the seventh grade, she achieved a class ranking for the very first time. This accomplishment was not attributable to any specific subject in which she excelled, as there was no subject in which she lagged behind.

And now she was the same as the other children, or rather, not the same. She was considered one of the top student in her class, because of which all the students began to interact with her.

Samantha made three best friends, the forever kind, who remained in contact with her even after leaving school and Samantha never made another best friend after those three until the nineteen years of Samantha. Within the class, Samantha and her three companions generally held dominion over academic achievement, their position at the fore shifting fluidly amongst themselves.

All of Samantha's friends, with one exception, are skilled in sports. While one friend focuses on Kabaddi, Samantha's talent extend to Kho-Kho, Throw ball, Kabaddi, and athletics. Once in a Hubli level competition, Samantha saved her team in Kho-Kho and won the medal. Since then, Samantha has become even more well-known in Kho-Kho.

By this juncture, Samantha's reputation within the school had reached considerable heights, and she was known to all her instructors as "Sahu ji". Samantha was made the captain of her school's Kho-Kho team for the inter school competition. In the inter school competition, Samantha achieved first position in the 100 meter race, first position in the long jump, first position in Kho- Kho, second position in Kabaddi, and third position in Throw ball.

Samantha loved nature deeply. She found great joy in towering mountains, flowing rivers, vast skies, the sun, the moon, villages, cities, trees, greenery and everything around her. She always immersed herself fully in the moment, feeling everything deeply. Samantha was a deep thinking individual who cherished her alone time. She loved to ponder life mysteries and found great comfort in the simple pleasure of music.

Samantha used to do all her work by herself and was a self-starter who believed in achieving her goals independent without burdening others. And she was unable to refuse any request of others for any work.

One day, while scrolling through her mobile, Samantha watched a video about the power and status of an IAS officer. After that, she researches about it and learns that she can also achieve this position with her hard work. She only thought that she would do it, but she didn't know how.

In 2019, the corona virus arrived and changed the routine of the entire world. Corona virus cases started appearing in India as well, due to which a lockdown was imposed. Schools and all workplaces were closed, and it had a huge impact on everyone financially as well as mentally. During the lockdown, everyone's life was very painful, sad, but Samantha's life was very enjoyable. Before the lockdown Samantha's elder sister and her cousin sister had both come to Sakleshpur. Throughout the lockdown, Samantha and her family enjoyed a lot. They tried many new dishes like pizza, Manchurian, jalebi, falooda, and many more at home during the lockdown. Samantha used to watch a south movie every day with her sisters at the time of lockdown. Samantha watched more than 70 to 80 south Indian movies. But she didn't know the name of even one of them except one or two.

They all used to go for a morning walk in the field next to their house, and it was during this time that Samantha learned to ride a scooty. But in reality, she got the scooty to ride only after her 12th grade.

For a year, when Samantha was in 9th grade, studied had completely stopped and there was no hope of schools reopening because the cases of corona were increasing. Because of the lockdown, they were unable to go to Jhansi for a long time, otherwise they used to go to Jhansi every four to five months.

Finally, the lockdown ended and Samantha's family planned to go to Jhansi with full preparation like gloves, masks, and a very big plastic sheet which they were going to use to cover their train cabin because during the corona time, curtains were not provided in trains. They were very excited and happy to go home. They stay in a separate house in Jhansi for 11 days, away from everyone else, so that if they have any diseases, it does not spread to others.

On the 12th day, when it was Krishna Janmashtami, they came to the house and celebrated Janmashtami very well. But in the evening her grandfather suddenly started breathing heavily. Her entire family became very panic. They tried to get the oxygen cylinder arranged as soon as possible, but not a single oxygen cylinder was found. Her uncle picked up her grandfather and took him to the hospital, but her grandfather had passed out before being taken to the hospital. The revelation struck like a bolt from the blue, leaving the entire family reeling in stunned silence. And suddenly everyone started crying. No one in the house could believe that grandfather was no more, especially her grandmother.

This period presented an exceptionally arduous trial for her family, compounded by the pervasive shadow of the ongoing pandemic, which served only to intensify their hardship.

Her grandfather was a very noble man, his death was mourned not only by his family but also by the entire neighborhood because he was very supportive of everyone, it did not matter to him whether they were family or outsiders, whoever was in trouble, he helped them.

Gradually, her family recovered and now they have moved back to Sakleshpur.

Now this time it was Samantha's tenth and also boards. Samantha was scared because of Kannada because her Kannada was not that much good for boards.

But Samantha enjoyed and worked the hardest in 10th grade, more than any other year in her entire school life.

Classes for 10th grade started online due to the pandemic in the initial months. However, the school reopened after two or three months. And then her teacher quickly completed the syllabus so that if the pandemic were to return, the syllabus would be completed. But after that, the pandemic completely ended and didn't return.

Finally, school life resumed after a long wait since the pandemic.

This year, a sports competition is being held between students from her school and another branch located in Mysore. She and all her friends except one went to Mysore by bus, which was a five hour journey. She enjoyed it very much with her friends in the bus. Also she stayed there for one night in a hostel. In that hostel, three members were allowed in one room, and Samantha's group also had three members. Samantha was the first girl in her family to not only go on a trip but also stayed overnight.

A competition was scheduled for the next day, contested between the students of the two respective branches.

2022/

Samantha's school's Kho-Kho team was very strong compared to other branch team. And Samantha's school's Kho-Kho team emerged victorious and they received medals and trophies.

Their trip to Mysore was successful, and they enjoyed themselves immensely on the way back as well.

Samantha used to wake up at 5 AM every morning and get ready to go to coaching by bicycle with her friend. After returning from coaching at 7; 30, she would quickly get ready and go to school in a taxi at 8 AM. And all day would study at school generally school got over at 4PM but because of the boards extra classes were held until 6PM. They got a 15minutes break at 4PM, during which time they would sit in the corridor, tease each other, and chat a lot. After returning home at 6PM. Samantha would study for the next stage test until 10 or 11 at night. And she also had to give extra time for Kannada language as well.

The days was very hard for her. She felt very light while sleeping at night after a whole day. They had to attend extra classes even on Sunday.

Once, during extra classes on a Sunday, the teacher didn't bring the key to the main gate, so they all jumped over the gate and went inside. Those days were very memorable and very precious for Samantha.

Through diligent efforts, Samantha achieved the highest marks on the Kannada pre-board examination. Her teacher subsequently addressed the class, urging them to emulate Samantha's example. She pointed out that despite Kannada not being Samantha's native language, her hand writing was exemplary, her score in Kannada was the highest, and her spoken Kannada was remarkably proficient.

Every time before the board exams, students used to get seven days holiday for Self Study, but this time, sir refused to give them the holiday. So, Samantha just cried because she really wanted that time to read the Kannada subject properly. And at that time, she cried in front of the teacher, and the teacher only gave Samantha the holiday for those seven days. The teacher didn't give the holiday to all the students. And in this way, Samantha scored 121 out of 125 in Kannada, and overall, she got 97% in her boards. But Samantha had absolutely no idea how this score and her hard word would be useful to her later in life.

THREE

A JOURNEY BACK TO JHANSI

Samantha's father was about to be transferred, so Samantha came to Jhansi earlier so that her studies would not be affected in 11 class. Now was the time for the Samantha to decide which stream and which school to join in Jhansi. Samantha was also excited to meet her old friends.

During the summer, Samantha started preparation for the UPSC exam because she was very excited to begin and enjoyed reading the subjects covered in the UPSC syllabus. She was also considering choosing the humanities stream in 11th grade but her sisters said that taking the science stream would be very useful, so she took the science [PCM] stream.

Samantha now lived in a joint family with her grandmother, uncle and aunt, and her elder aunt and uncle. Although Samantha liked living with her family, she also enjoyed spending time alone, enjoying the peace and quiet.

And she was thinking a lot about the UPSC exam. Since the 7th grade, Samantha had dreamed of becoming an IAS officer.

Samantha got admission in a school in Jhansi and she started going school. But she saw that there was no proper study in the schools here, if you want to complete the syllabus, you have to join coaching. And there also, only the syllabus is completed, you have to do the practice yourself, you have to prepare for the exam yourself everything had to be done there by yourself. And Samantha, who was completely dependent on teachers in her previous school, found it very difficult to do everything by herself and she didn't have any friends to ask anything there. She noticed that every girl there was very proud and boastful and lying. Her social circle was very small, and those friends were not very close; they were just for the sake of talking.

Samantha also joined coaching, but she didn't understand much there, then she started studying online and slowly it took her the whole year to understand. She used to curse the school system here a lot.

She thought that if she had taken humanities, it would have been more useful, as she had an interest in those subjects. She was not able to focus on her science stream because she was more attracted to UPSC, sometimes she would even read arts subjects. But because of this, she felt very sad that she was not able to study well. Sometimes she would even cry, but Samantha never cried in front of anyone. She always cried alone, and only when she couldn't handle her emotions would she cry in front of everyone, which was very rare. And when she was very emotional, she couldn't even speak.

Samantha has now learned to realize everything after a full year, she realized that everything is happening according to her, just as she thinks, and even better than that. Samantha came to Jhansi and she learned to handle everything by herself, to do it herself, which is very important skill for UPSC and perhaps she couldn't have learned that by living there. The situation she faced were making Samantha stronger, and now she was developing a positive approach towards everything.

She also missed her parents, friends, her old house, the time she spend there, the environment, the fun and the struggles, and she could not bring that time back.

Samantha was a very quiet girl, and her face was always smiling. She always thought, "keep silence to avoid the problems, keep smile to solve the problems". She was an exceptionally good listener, always carefully considering what others had said before responding.

She recalled a sentiment she had encountered elsewhere-"A listening ear is a loving heart".

Samantha commenced her 12th grade studies with renewed vigor. Having thoroughly analyzed the preceding year's experiences, she was determined not to replicate past errors. Her academic approach was now characterized by clarity and focus. She felt like 12th grade would end soon and she would start preparing for UPSC. At this time, she had clearly thought that she was going to do BA after 12th and UPSC preparation along with it.

With a lot of patience and hard work, she scored 80% in 12th grade by herself, while her other friends in Karnataka got 95 to 97%. But she was satisfied with it because she did it herself, and most importantly, she learned the skill of learning independently.

Samantha, once she set her mind on doing something, she would do it. She had self confidence in herself. She knew how vast the UPSC syllabus was, and she had decided to pursue it as early as 7th grade. However, at that time, even the small 7th grade syllabus seemed huge to her. But even then, she resolved that she would do it no matter what. She would face any problems that came her way and would definitely succeed.

Samantha did not like to tell anyone about anything, she always kept everything to herself.

Samantha's father was her greatest inspiration. He supported her in everything she did, granting her considerable freedom. Samantha constantly strove to make her parents proud, and she achieved this at every possible turn because she thinks success is not a point to reach it's a journey of learning something new in every step of the life and make yourself and others proud. It filled her with joy whenever her father beamed with pride at having her as his daughter.

Samantha didn't even take a break after boards, she started preparing for UPSC and now she can finally focus on it completely.

FOUR

SAMANTHA'S EARLY CAREER AT 19

Samantha always preferred studying in peace and solitude, but she couldn't focus well in her joint family. Full focus is essential for UPSC preparation, requiring 7 or 8 hours of study, but more importantly, a conducive environment for 24 hours. This is because when we memorize something, we tend to remind ourselves of it frequently when alone. However, amidst many people, we engage in various conversation, increasing the chances of forgetting. Being alone allows for deeper thinking and better self-discovery.

Samantha is looking for a BA private program that will give her more time to prepare for her exams.

Samantha and her mother just after the boards, both went back to Karnataka because Samantha's father was not yet transferred.

And this was very good for Samantha because she could study very well there alone. She may be able to focus better without the distractions of being around other people.

Samantha had a strong belief that if you truly desire something from the depths of your heart, the entire universe conspires to help you achieve it. And this is exactly what was happening with Samantha, everything was going according to her.

Samantha from Karnataka decided to pursue self-study, believing in her ability to succeed through this method, and she dedicated two or three months to it.

Once, Samantha opened the website of a coaching institution to check questions. She received a call from the coaching center, and they spoke to her father. They explained everything in detail, and her father suggested that she join the coaching as it would be more beneficial for her studies and allows her to follow a proper timetable.

However, it was a bit costly, so Samantha was contemplating whether or not to take it. But then, Samantha thought that it would create a bit more pressure for her preparation, and she ended up enrolling in the batch.

Samantha's father understood her unsaid words, and if she ever said something, he would definitely get it for her. Samantha's father would get her everything she needed, be it a laptop, board, or phone, as soon as she asked for it, because they trust her very much.

One day, a vacancy was announced based on 10th grade merit for those who are 18 plus. Samantha's father asked her to fill out the form, but she had no interest in it. However, she filled it out anyway but her entire focus was on the UPSC exam.

Her father constantly used to check the results. At that time she was in Jhansi. Samantha was not selected in the first merit list. And also not selected in the second merit list. Then, Samantha returned to Karnataka a day before her birthday.

And in the third merit list, Samantha's name appeared, and that day was also her birthday. She got a more beautiful gift on her birthday. But in reality, she was not that excited because she knew that this would have some effect on her UPSC preparation.

The following day, subsequent to her birthday, she journeyed once more to Jhansi for the purpose of verification. Samantha had never even imagined that she would get a job because of her 10th class result. For her, it was a completely unexpected and sudden event.

She was selected for GDS, a position with a Salary ranging from rupees 15,000 to 17,000. Her entire family was against her taking the job, saying that it wasn't right for girls to work for such a low salary, especially in a village and at such a young age.

Even though Samantha's father had a very high salary, he still encouraged her to take the job because he felt it would make her independent. He believed that money wasn't the most important thing; what matter was that she would become an independent young girl, and that she could also continue her studies alongside the job.

Samantha always obeyed her father, and he had told her that if she couldn't manage her studies with the job, she could quit. However, quitting before even trying would be like refusing a good opportunity.

So, Samantha joined the job in December. And this is how Samantha started her early career at 19.

FIVE

SAMANTHA – A LIFE IN MOTION

Samantha's life was now going on with UPSC preparation along with the job, but in the beginning, she faced many problems in the job. She gradually learned her work, but her group people were very kind; they were very supportive of Samantha in everything she did.

Samantha's mother always used to travel with her. First, she stayed with her in banglore with her father. Then, she stayed with her in Jhansi. Now, due to Samantha's job, she has to stay with her. Though she didn't like living anywhere except Jhansi. Samantha's mother also went through a lot of struggles. Amidst all this, Samantha's father had also learned to cook because his transfer had not yet happened and he was living alone there.

Among all these people, Samantha observed that the villages are very kind, trustworthy, and good-hearted. They shower unconditional love. She also observed that although some villages consume alcohol or tobacco products like gutka, they are still very kind people. She had never seen such kind people in cities, because there, if someone consumes alcohol or gutka, they are considered to be bad people. However, in villages, even those who do these things are very, very kind people.

Samantha's observations extended beyond the immediate demands of her work. Her position provided a rich tapestry of experience, from which she gleaned a multitude of lessons, far surpassing the simple acquisition of job-related skills.

At last, "Behind every progressive daughter there is a progressive father and even moms". Samantha has not yet attained her objective, but her parents has been a constant source of support throughout her journey. They have been instrumental in her every significant achievement.

[THE BOOK WILL CONTINUE IN THE NEXT PART.]

Everything is beautiful,
When you start looking in a good way.
Everything is useful,
When you start running your mind.
Everyone is good,
When your heart is pure.
Everyone is trustable,
When you first start trusting others.
Everything is perfect,
When you think it is perfect.
It's completely depends on you for yourself.
- Vandana sahu

www.ingramcontent.com/pod-product-compliance
Lightning Source LLC
La Vergne TN
LVHW041304150826
845673LV00008B/2718

* 9 7 9 8 8 9 7 2 4 4 3 5 5 *